A Pile of Pigs

by Judith Ross Enderle
and Stephanie Gordon Tessler

illustrated by Charles Jordan

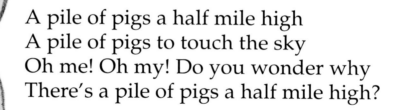

A pile of pigs a half mile high
A pile of pigs to touch the sky
Oh me! Oh my! Do you wonder why
There's a pile of pigs a half mile high?

BELL BOOKS
BOYDS MILLS PRESS

Published by Bell Books
Boyds Mills Press, Inc.
A Highlights Company
910 Church Street
Honesdale, Pennsylvania 18431

Publisher Cataloging-in-Publication Data
Enderle, Judith Ross.
    A pile of pigs / by Judith Ross Enderle and Stephanie Gordon Tessler ;
illustrated by Charles Jordan.
[24] p. : col. ill. ; cm.
Summary: Following his curiosity, littlest pig has all the pigs form a high
pyramid to look over the other side of the barn.
ISBN 1-878093-88-6
1. Swine—Fiction—Juvenile literature. [1. Swine—Fiction.] I. Tessler, Stephanie
Gordon. II. Jordan, Charles, ill. III. Title.
    [E]   1993
Library of Congress Catalog Card Number: 91-77620

First edition, 1993
The text of this book is set in 16-point Palatino.
The illustrations are done with colored pencils.
Distributed by St. Martin's Press
Printed in Hong Kong

10 9 8 7 6 5 4 3 2 1

For Kent, Clay, Marileta, and the rest of
the gang back at the farm. And for
Connie, who started it all.
—J.R.E. & S.G.T.

For Peggy.
—C. J.

Strut-a-doodle doo! Strut-a-doodle doo!
"You should see what the cows are doing,"
crowed Rooster.

"What are the cows doing?" asked Littlest Pig.
"Those cows aren't doing a thing." Grandpa Pig
grunted and closed his eyes.

Littlest Pig got snout to snout with Grandpa.
"What if the cows *are* doing something?"
Grandpa opened one eye. "Don't care," he grunted.
And he rolled over into the mud.

From behind the sty rails, Littlest Pig watched Rooster strut away. And there, between Grandpa's whiskers and Mama's tail, he spied the old circus poster on the side of the barn.

Littlest Pig scampered from pig to pig to pig.
"Super duper," he began. "Pigalini Brothers,"
he added. "Skyscraper," he went on.
"Pyramid," he finished.
The other pigs were excited.
"We'll see the whole world," they said.

"We'll find out what the cows are doing,"
Littlest Pig said.
Only Grandpa Pig wasn't excited.
"Those cows aren't doing a thing,"
grunted Grandpa Pig.
Littlest Pig got snout to snout with Grandpa.
"I want to see for myself," he said.

And so did Grandma Pig, Uncle Parsnip, and Aunt Penelope Pig, Cousins Percy, Preston, Patsy, Paulette, Puffer, Poe, and Pandora Pig. Even Mama and Papa Pig wanted to know what the cows were doing. So they all agreed to help Littlest Pig make a Super Duper Pig Pyramid. But not Grandpa Pig. He grunted and rolled over into the mud.

PIG
BY PIG BY PIG
BY PIG BY PIG BY PIG
BY PIG BY PIG BY PIG BY PIG BY PIG
the pyramid grew and grew and grew.

"Climb faster, Littlest Pig. We can almost see the cows," called the two topmost pigs.
Littlest Pig scrambled from shoulder to snout, from snout to shoulder, from pig part to pig part.

The bottom pigs moaned.
The pyramid swayed back.
The pyramid swayed forth.

The middle pigs groaned.
The pyramid swayed left.
The pyramid swayed right.

"Ooomph," said the two topmost pigs, as the
Littlest Pig balanced on their shoulders.
"What are the cows doing?" shouted all the pigs.
"I can't see yet," called Littlest Pig.

Then the Littlest Pig balanced on the two
topmost pigs' snouts.
"What are the cows doing?" shouted all the pigs.
"I can't see yet," called Littlest Pig.

Then the Littlest Pig balanced on his tiptoes
on the tiptop of the two topmost pigs' heads.
The pyramid swayed back.
The pyramid swayed forth.
The pyramid swayed left.
The pyramid swayed right.

"I can see them! I can see them," shouted Littlest Pig.
"What are the cows doing?" shouted all the pigs.
Just as the pyramid wobbled and bobbled and—

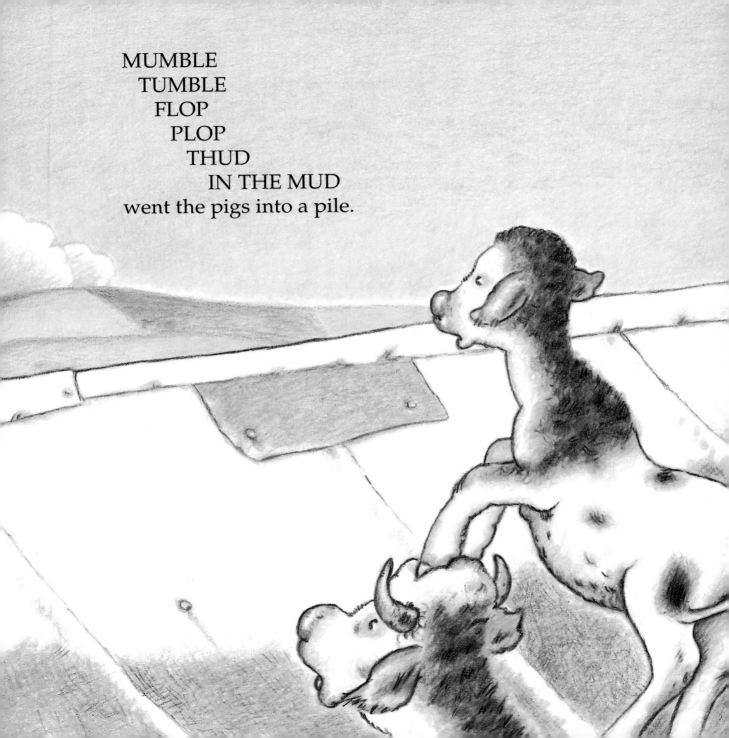

MUMBLE
TUMBLE
FLOP
PLOP
THUD
IN THE MUD
went the pigs into a pile.

Littlest Pig rubbed his rump.
"What were the cows doing?"
asked all the pigs.
"They were making a pyramid.
They were looking at us,"
said Littlest Pig.
Grandpa Pig grunted and
rolled over into the mud.

Strut-a-doodle-doo! Strut-a-doodle doo!
"You should see what the sheep are doing,"
crowed Rooster.
Littlest Pig grunted and rolled over into the mud—
next to Grandpa.